MEET WILD BOARS

MEET WILD BOARS

MEG ROSOFF AND SOPHIE BLACKALL

PUFFIN

PUFFIN BOOKS

Published by the Penguin Group
Penguin Books Ltd, 80 Strand, London WC2R 0RL, England
Penguin Group (USA) Inc., 375 Hudson Street, New York, New York 10014, USA
Penguin Group (Canada), 90 Eglinton Avenue East, Suite 700, Toronto, Ontario, Canada M4P 2Y3 (a division of Pearson Penguin Canada Inc.)
Penguin Ireland, 25 St Stephen's Green, Dublin 2, Ireland (a division of Penguin Books Ltd)
Penguin Group (Australia), 250 Camberwell Road, Camberwell, Victoria 3124, Australia (a division of Pearson Australia Group Pty Ltd)
Penguin Books India Pvt Ltd, 11 Community Centre, Panchsheel Park, New Delhi – 110 017, India
Penguin Group (NZ), cnr Airborne and Rosedale Roads, Albany, Auckland 1310, New Zealand (a division of Pearson New Zealand Ltd)
Penguin Books (South Africa) (Pty) Ltd, 24 Sturdee Avenue, Rosebank, Johannesburg 2196, South Africa

Penguin Books Ltd, Registered Offices: 80 Strand, London WC2R 0RL, England

www.penguin.com

First published in the United States by Henry Holt and Company, LLC 2005
First published in Great Britain in Puffin Books 2005
Published in this edition 2006

10 9 8 7 6 5 4 3 2 1

Text copyright © Meg Rosoff, 2005
Illustrations copyright © Sophie Blackall, 2005
All rights reserved

The moral right of the author and illustrator has been asserted

Set in Old Claude
Handlettering by Sophie Blackall
Manufactured in China

British Library Cataloguing in Publication Data
A CIP catalogue record for this book is available from the British Library

ISBN-13: 978–0–141–50038–6
ISBN-10: 0–141–50038–7

For Gloria (who invented Wild Boars)
— M. R.

For Nick, the funniest man I know
— S. B.

BORIS

MORRIS

HORACE

DORIS

This is Boris.

This is Morris.

This is Horace.

This is Doris.

They are wild boars.

They are
dirty and smelly,
bad-tempered and rude.
Do you like them?

Never mind.

They do not like you either.

If you are polite to Boris and hold the door for him he will tusk you with his horrible tusks.

TUSK TUSK TUSK.

Bad Boris.

STOMP
STOMP
STOMP

If you share your treats with Morris
he will stomp on them with his beastly feet.

STOMP STOMP STOMP

Naughty Morris.

If you try to help Horace with his mittens
he will make a nasty smell and snort with laughter.

SNORT SNORT SNORT

Horrid Horace.

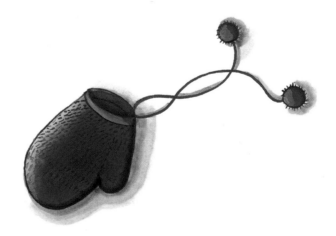

And as for Doris –
oh, my my.

She is STINKIER than a stinkpot turtle.

She is UGLIER than an Ugli fruit.

She is BOSSIER than a Bossysaurus.

Poor wild boars.
Nobody loves them.

Maybe just once they could come to your house.

You could make them some snacks.

You might show them your toys.

Play dress-up or dominoes.

Splash in the bath.

They could borrow pyjamas
and sleep in your room.

Nice wild boars.
Sweet wild boars.
They promise
just this once
they will try to be good.

OH NO THEY WILL NOT.

Horace will soak in the toilet for hours

he'll eat all your soap

clip his toenails in bed

be rude to your pets

cut the strings off your puppets

make fun of your feet

lock himself in the shed.

Morris won't eat what you give him for supper

or let you go first

say excuse me

or please.

He'll sneer and he'll scratch

stick his snout up your jumper

then eat all your chocolate

and give you his fleas.

Boris will break every one of your pencils

he'll smash up your puzzles

and use all your glue

make horrible smells

leave the tops off your pens

stamp his foot

have a tantrum

then swear it was you.

And as for Doris
(who has never been good,
not for one single second,
not once
not ever
never)
she will ask for a toy in case she gets
lonely and scared in the dark.
Dear little Doris!

To which we say

HA!

Given half a chance

(or even less)

Doris will eat your very best whale,

flippers and all.

So perhaps it is best if we all agree
that there is no such thing as a nice wild boar.

Then if you happen to run across one
that is fluffy and sweet
(though chances are that you won't)
you will be very pleasantly amazed.

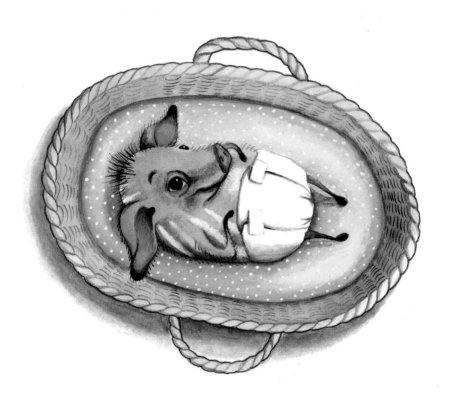

But not at all fooled.

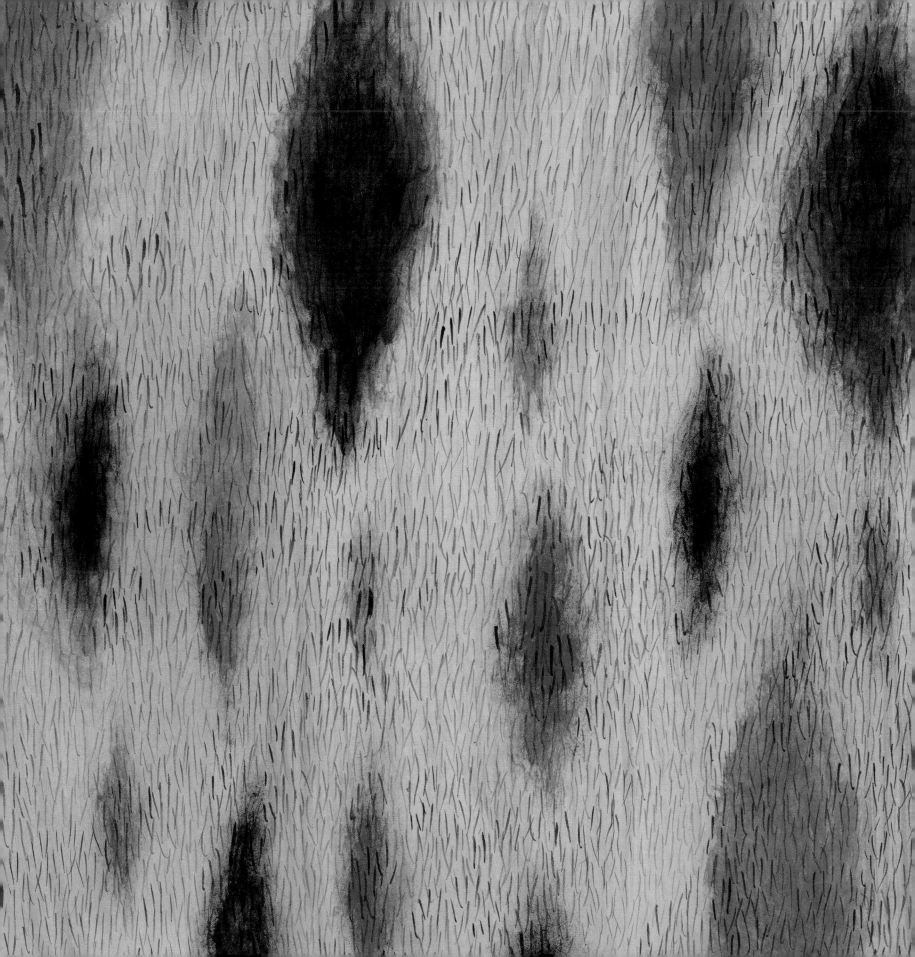